Scrooge
#worstgiftever

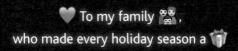

To my family, who made every holiday season a 🎁

Text copyright © 2016 by Penguin Random House LLC
Emoji copyright © Apple Inc.
Image on page 3 © Shutterstock/Ollyy; pages 24 and 26 © Shutterstock/mRGB;
page 99 man © Shutterstock/Kiselev Andrey Valerevich,
house © Shutterstock/Shelli Jensen, sign © Shutterstock/Andy Dean Photography

All rights reserved. Published in the United States by Random House Children's Books,
a division of Penguin Random House LLC, New York.

Random House and the colophon are registered trademarks of
Penguin Random House LLC.

Visit us on the Web! randomhouseteens.com

Educators and librarians, for a variety of teaching tools,
visit us at RHTeachersLibrarians.com

Library of Congress Cataloging-in-Publication Data
Names: Wright, Brett, author. | Dickens, Charles, 1812–1870. Christmas carol.
Title: Scrooge #worstgiftever / Charles Dickens and Brett Wright.
Description: First edition. | New York : Random House, [2016] | Summary: A miser learns
the true meaning of Christmas when three ghostly visitors review his
past and foretell his future. Text accompanied by emojis.
Identifiers: LCCN 2015030065 | ISBN 978-0-399-55064-5 (hardcover) |
ISBN 978-0-399-55065-2 (ebook)
Subjects: | CYAC: Christmas—Fiction. | Ghosts—Fiction. | Great Britain—History—
19th century—Fiction. | Social media—Fiction.
Classification: LCC PZ7.1.W75 Sc 2016 | DDC [Fic]—dc23
LC record available at http://lccn.loc.gov/20150300

MANUFACTURED IN CHINA
10 9 8 7 6 5 4 3 2 1
First Edition

Scrooge

#worstgiftever

charles dickens

+

Brett wright

Random House 🏠 New York

who's who

 Scrooge

 Marley

 Fred, Scrooge's **nephew**

 Fred's Wife

 Ghost of Christmas Past

 Ghost of Christmas Present

 Ghost of Christmas Yet to Come

 Bob Cratchit

 Mrs. Cratchit

 Martha Cratchit

 Belinda Cratchit

 Peter Cratchit

 Tiny Tim Cratchit

Send

📱 Unknown Number #1, 555-6650

📱 Unknown Number #2, 555-5586

📱 Unknown Number #3, 555-1422

👩‍🦳 Mrs. Dilber, Scrooge's housekeeper

👴 Old Joe, buys Scrooge's old possessions

👗 Laundress, former employee of Scrooge

💀 Undertaker

👫 Husband and Wife

🍗 Grocer

Send

Chapter 1

Christmas Eve

Jacob Marley is dead. 😵
Dead as a doornail. 🚪🔨
As stated in Mr. Marley's will 📃,
he leaves his estate 🏠 to
Ebenezer Scrooge 👨.

Yes, you read that correctly. 😨 Mr. Marley's
business partner, Mr. Scrooge—whose 🤍 is as cold
as ❄️—has signed the papers 📝 declaring
Mr. Marley's death.

Mr. Scrooge will continue to operate their
business 💰💰 under both names and shows no
signs of slowing down.

Not even for Christmas tomorrow.
🚫🎅🎄🎁⛄🚫

Send

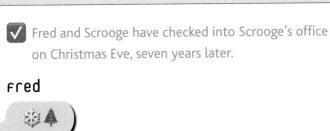

☑ Fred and Scrooge have checked into Scrooge's office on Christmas Eve, seven years later.

Fred

scrooge

Fred

scrooge

Fred

scrooge

Fred

MERRY CHRISTMAS, UNCLE SCROOGE!

Send

scrooge

I knew that's where this was going. BAH!

fred

Aw, lighten up! It's CHRISTMAS EVE. The best time of the year!

scrooge

HAMBURGER.

Hmph! HAM BUG.

#autocorrectfail

HUMBUG.

I haaate Christmas.

fred

You don't mean that.

scrooge

You bet your sweet , I do. What's there to like about this holiday?

Send

scrooge

First of all, it leaves you broke.

Second, it means you're a year older. 🐵

And third, WHO CARES? I wouldn't mind at all if there was never another stupid Christmas again. 😷

fred

😳

That is , and you know it! It's a wonderful time. Maybe the only time of year when people are actually nice and full of love 🤍 for others.

scrooge

💔💔💔

fred

You're impossible. 😔

The whole reason I reached out to you is to invite you to dinner <u>tomorrow</u>.

Send

scrooge

No ty. I would rather dine with the devil 😈 than visit your 🏠.

fred

Ooooookay. Little harsh. Why?

scrooge

Why did you get married? 👰🤵

fred

Because I fell in love. 💘

scrooge

HA! Love! 😂 That's the only thing in this 🌍 more ridiculous than Christmas.

fred

That's why you're not coming? 😦

scrooge

Hmph.👀

Send

Fred

Whatever, Uncle Scrooge. ✌️ Invitation still stands if you change your mind. 💌

scrooge

I. Won't.

Fred

🎄🎁 Merry Christmas! 🎁🎄

scrooge

Fred

And a HAPPY NEW YEAR too, ya old grouch! 😜

● ● ●

Group text: 555-6650, Scrooge, 555-5586

555-6650

hi!! 👋 is this scrooge and marley's??

scrooge

WTF. Who's this?

How'd you get my number?

555-5586

r we speaking 2 scrooge or marley??

scrooge

Marley's been dead 💀 for seven years exactly <u>tonight</u>, so I'll give you two guesses and the first one doesn't count. 😝

555-6650

oh, great!! we're from a charity that mr. marley used to donate to ALL the time. 📩 knowing that it's the anniversary of his untimely death 😔, we're sure that you'll want to donate as generously as he did, mr. scrooge! 💰 💳 perhaps in his name??

555-5586

& now is the perfect time of yr 2 donate. 🗓 so many ppl can barely get by as it is & that can b esp hard @ xmas. 🐱

Send

scrooge

BAH! 😠 There are PLENTY of places for those people to go. 👇 👇 👈 👉

I am NOT one of them!

Ever heard of prisons? Workhouses?

555-6650

but, sir!! we just want to bring some warmth and good cheer to those who need them. 😄 now, how much can i put you down for? ✒️

scrooge

NADA.

555-5586

u want 2 b anon? that's cool! 😃

scrooge

No! 😠 I want 2 b left alone.

Adding you both to the Do Not Call list. TTYN.

Send

● ● ●

ʙoʙ cratcʜit

Um. 😣 Mr. Scrooge?

scrooge

OH, WHAT NOW??

ʙoʙ cratcʜit

😓 Um, um, um. I was just wondering if it would be OK to take <u>tomorrow</u> off? So I can spend Christmas with my family? 👨‍👩‍👧

scrooge

Lemme guess. You expect me to give you a paid holiday too? 😒

ʙoʙ cratcʜit

It's only one day of the year. . . .

scrooge

Don't remind me. 😼 Every <u>December 25</u>.

Fine. But you better be here EXTRA early the next day to make up for it. 🕐

Send

Bob Cratchit

😍 Yes, sir, I promise! Thank you! Merry Christmas!

scrooge

Bah HUMMINGBIRD.

OMG. 😡 Adding a shortcut to my keyboard.

Bah humbug! 😷

😈 Scrooge

I. HATE. CHRISTMAS! 😠 I 🙏 that someday we live in a 🌍 where we don't celebrate such a lousy holiday. 🚫 🎄 🎅 🚫 #BahHumbug

👍 Be the first to like this.   REPLY

Scrooge: I'm going to bed, and I hope I 😴 through this entire week! 😡

● ● ●

Marley

boo

Send

scrooge

👀

Who is this? zzZ Do you have any idea what time it is?

marley

bOOooOOooOOoo

scrooge

😠 Stop messing with me!

marley

i think u mean, who WAS this? 😜

scrooge

🙂 Fine. Who WAS this?

And how did YOU get my 📱 number? I swear I'm unlisted!

marley

it's me, ebz! jake! jacob marley. 👋

Send

scrooge

I don't believe you.

marley

i'll send a selfie.

#nofilter

scrooge

What? This is ridiculous. I've gone mad. 🌀🌀

Buzz off. 🐝

marley

i'll prove it.

ur wearing a robe 🧥 4 bed rn. 😴

scrooge

😟 How do you know that?

Send

marley

weeelll, i'm kind of a 👻 so i can still 👀 u.

i've been watchin u 4 a while now. 📅

scrooge

Really? Um. What's it like to be ... dead? 😵

marley

not so gr8 tbh w/u.

i've got all these ⛓️ ⛓️ ⛓️ covering me. #OOTD #NAGL

scrooge

Why?

marley

it's my own fault. 😔

i'm locked up 🔓 bc of how i acted when i was alive.

scrooge

That's outrageous! 😤 Because you were a successful businessman? 💰 💲 💰 💲 💰

Send

marley

that's just it—i worked 2 much, ebz.

📅 17 📅 17 📅 17 📅 17 📅 17 📅 17 📅 17

i never left our office 2 rly LIVE & b w/ppl i cared abt.

scrooge

I can't believe you're being punished for all the good you did....

marley

i didn't do as much good 4 others as i did 4 myself. i shouldabin leaving the office on time 🕐, volunteering 🏢 & rly helping ppl. 😇

not just taking shortcuts ✂️ by donating dough 💵💰 & believing that was enuf 2 make up 4 my selfishness.

now i'm basically screwed. 👻 forced 2 roam 🌍 w/out peace n quiet.

scrooge

😱

Send

marley

ya, total bummer . . .

buuut . . .

here's . . .

the . . .

thing . . .

•••

hello?!

scrooge

What? I'm listening. 👂

marley

oh, that was supposed 2 b suspenseful but whatevz. 💁

there's still hope 4 u, ebz, so u don't end up like me.
🚫 ☠ 🚫

Send

scrooge

Whaddya mean?

marley

yer gonna b visited by 3 spirits 👻 👻 👻 . . .

scrooge

PASS. I choose to end up like you. NBD. 💊 💀 💊

marley

. . . 4 the next 3 nights.

scrooge

Aw, C'MON! 😫 Can't they visit me all at once and get it over with?

marley

the 1st spirit will show up @ 1 tomorrow. 🕐

2 days l8r, the 2nd will come at the same time. 🕐

& on the 3rd nite, the last spirit will visit you at midnight. 🕛

Send

scrooge

Should I be writing this down?

Marley

u won't hear from me again after 2nite, ebz. 😞

so remember what i said.

gl2u!!

Send

Chapter 2
Ghost of Christmas Past

ghost of christmas past

W

Ak

E

WaK

GAH. 😠

scrooge

Um, hi? 🙁

ghost of christmas past

Wakey, wakey!

Sry about that. I'm still getting used 2 this thing. 📱

Plus, my fingers are way 2 big for this. 👎

N-e-way. Wakey, wakey, Scrooge! ⏰

scrooge

😴 Who is this?

ghost of christmas past

Ghost of Christmas Past, at ur service. 👻 🎄

The ultimate #tbt and #fbf. 😉

scrooge

That's impossible. I literally just fell asleep! zzᶻ

ghost of christmas past

Did u LITERALLY just fall asleep? Like LITERALLY? 😜

scrooge

😠 YES!

And Jacob said you wouldn't be here until <u>tomorrow</u>.
I couldn't have slept through an entire day. ⌚

ghost of christmas past

IDK what to tell u. It's on the dot. And we don't
have a lot of time, so let's get to saving u! 😃

scrooge

😒 You can save me by letting me sleep more.

Send

ghost of christmas past

UP!

I'm ur past, Scroogey. And I got some 💩 to show u that ur probs not gonna like. 👀

scrooge

Maybe I'll take a rain check. ⛱ ✔

ghost of christmas past

Nice try. Follow me! 🏃

scrooge

But I'm not a 👻. I can't just reappear somewhere else like you can.

ghost of christmas past

No problemo! 😌 Just tap this.

Send

ghost of christmas past

Did u tap it?

scrooge

What? Of course! 👆

ghost of christmas past

Try again. Don't think it worked.

scrooge

😠

Fine! There.

ghost of christmas past

Nope. Didn't work. Sorry, it's this app. Pictures disappear after 10 seconds. ➖ 📷

Here u go.

Send

✓ Ghost of Christmas Past and Scrooge have checked
into the countryside.

Ghost of christmas past

Recognize this ?

scrooge

😩 I grew up here. This is my childhood home.

Ghost of christmas past

U OK, Scroogey?

scrooge

😥 I'm fine. I just have something in my eye.

Send

Ghost of Christmas Past

Mhm. 😏 So this is all familiar to u?

scrooge

Of course! I recognize everything. I remember these 🌲🌲🌲🌲 and the town ⛪. All these 🏠🏠🏠.

Ghost of Christmas Past

Interesting . . . seems u've forgotten most of these things in recent years. 😒

scrooge

😔

Look! 🐴👦🐴👦🐴👦 Let's go say hi!

Ghost of Christmas Past

Hold up. ✋ These are just IMAGES of ur past. U can't interact with em & they can't 👀 us either.

scrooge

😔

Ghost of Christmas Past

I want to show u the 🏢. Remember?

Send

scrooge

Boy, do I . . .

ghost of christmas past

Yes, speaking of . . . there's still one little 👦 in there, all alone. Neglected by his 👨‍👩‍👧 and friends.

scrooge

I know him very well. 🙀

ghost of christmas past

Look closer. 🔍 Whatcha see?

scrooge

He's reading. 📖

I mean, I'm reading.

ghost of christmas past

That's right. That's u. 👉

scrooge

Everyone else had gone home and I was still there with only my 📚. I loved those stories, though.

Send

scrooge

I just wish . . . ⭐

Ghost of christmas past

Wish what?

scrooge

Nothing. Only that, last night, there was a 👦 singing carols 🎶 🎵 outside my 🏠, and I wish I had given him something. That's all.

Ghost of christmas past

😃

Let's look at another Christmas year. Tap this.

✅ Ghost of Christmas Past and Scrooge have checked into the , years later.

Send

scrooge

Oh, no. 🙈 Why are you doing this to me?

ghost of christmas past

Technically, u did this to urself. 💡

scrooge

Yes. I was alone again. But this time my sister Fan 👧 came to take me 🏠. She said Father 👴 was nicer now, and I could return to spend Christmas together as a family. 🎅 🎁 👨‍👩‍👦

ghost of christmas past

U loved Fan 👧, didn't u?

scrooge

She had a tender heart.

ghost of christmas past

Had? 🙁 Past tense? Who r u—me? 😉

scrooge

You know as well as I do that she's dead. 😔

Send

ghost of christmas past

Shortly after she was grown and had a 👶, right?

scrooge

She had just gotten married 👰 and they had one child. 👨‍👧

ghost of christmas past

Ur nephew.

scrooge

My nephew. Fred. 😞

ghost of christmas past

I want to show u another place. 📍 Tap this.

JK not that 1!! Pretty cute tho, amirite? 😊 Heh.

Send

ghost of christmas past

This one:

✅ Ghost of Christmas Past and Scrooge have checked into Fezziwig's warehouse.

scrooge

My old apprenticeship! 🖨️ ☎️

There's my boss, Mr. Fezziwig! 👔 And my colleague and friend Dick Wilkins!

ghost of christmas past

What was Fezziwig like as a boss?

scrooge

He was so nice that year. 🎁 On Christmas Eve we closed early, and he brought in a musician to entertain us. 🎻

Then he brought his whole 👨‍👩‍👧 in and we had a party.

Send

scrooge

Ghost of christmas past

Wow! That must have cost a fortune.

scrooge

No, not at all! It was hardly anything. Fezziwig made us all so 😄 without spending much.

Ghost of christmas past

He had that sort of power?

scrooge

•••

Ghost of christmas past

U there?

scrooge

•••

Send

ghost of christmas past

WHAT ARE YOU SAYING? I ONLY SEE THAT YOU'RE TYPING!

EVERYTHING IS DOWN, UGH! 😖 WHAT'S THE WIFI PASSWORD? FAX ME? 📠

Gonna get in so much trouble 4 using all this data! 😫

scrooge

No, sorry. I didn't hit send yet. I was just thinking. 💭

ghost of christmas past

Oh, phew. Thought I'd lost u. 💀

(That dog is so cute.)

scrooge

I was thinking about Bob Cratchit. 😔

ghost of christmas past

Oh. Then hold on to ur bc we're not done yet.

U know what to do. Tap it!

Send

ghost of christmas past

✅ Ghost of Christmas Past and Scrooge have checked into Scrooge's 🏠, years later.

ghost of christmas past

This is the exact place where u once chitchatted w/a 💔👧.

scrooge

Oh, no. 🙁

ghost of christmas past

Oh, yes. It's Belle! 🔔

What happened there? U guys were cute. #OTP

scrooge

Belle. My #bae.

She claimed I something more than her. . . .

Send

Ghost of christmas past

Go on. And that was . . . ?

scrooge

Do I have to spell it out!? Money, of course. 💰 💵

I chose being rich over her. 💵 > 🖤

Ghost of christmas past

Why would u ever do that? 🙁

scrooge

I didn't want to be poor.

Ghost of christmas past

But she loved u even when u were both poor, didn't she? 💕

scrooge

Yes, but she said I changed after I made money. ✅
My only goal was my fortune.

Ghost of christmas past

🐵 Sounds like u rly blew that. 💣 ✨

Send

scrooge

She dumped me on the spot 📦 and called the wedding off. 🚫 💍

WHY are you torturing me with these memories? 😭

ghost of christmas past

I have 1 more thing to show u before my time runs out. ⏳

But ur not gonna like it. 😔

✅ Ghost of Christmas Past and Scrooge have checked into Belle's 🏠.

scrooge

You brought me to Belle's 🏠? Why?

ghost of christmas past

So u can 👀 what u gave up for 💰 💰.

Look over there, by the 🔥. See that 👧?

scrooge

😍 Belle looks as beautiful as ever.

ghost of christmas past

That's not Belle. 🚫 🔔 That's her daughter?

scrooge

Wait. 🙁 Are you asking or telling me?

ghost of christmas past

Oops!

I meant * * ! * * 😃

scrooge

She's a clone. 👯 To think she could have been . . .

ghost of christmas past

Urs?

scrooge

Send

ghost of christmas past

She's about to open 🎁 🎁 with her new .

scrooge

You are the WORST! 😠

Stop haunting me! I want you GONE. 👻 🔫

ghost of christmas past

Hey, NMF ¯_("/)_/¯

I didn't cause all these things. U did!

 And I'm only the first one u have to put up with.

(I'm rly getting the hang of this, don't u think?)

scrooge

BAH! I'm done. Blocking you. 🚫 📱

And going back to bed. 😴

● ● ●

Send

Scrooge

Having the craziest, worst dreams lately.
#wakemeupwhenChristmasends

 Be the first to like this.   REPLY

Send

Chapter 3

Ghost of Christmas Present

Send

ghost of christmas present

Knock, knock! 🚪

scrooge

It's already 🕐? That was quick. Ugh.

ghost of christmas present

Ahem. Knock, knock. 🚪

scrooge

What? Who's there?

ghost of christmas present

Donut. 🍩

scrooge

Uh, 🍩 who?

ghost of christmas present

DONUT open until Christmas! LOL. 🍩 🎁 🎄

scrooge

🙄

Send

scrooge

Bah. And who exactly are you?

ghost of christmas present

Just call me ~Ghost of Christmas Present~ 💀 🎁

Don'tcha luvvit, y/y? 😄

scrooge

Yeah, it's great, whatever.

ghost of christmas present

Well, sheesh. They told me you'd be , but I didn't realize the dial would be turned ALL the way ⬆️.

You are cranky AF.

They should call you Screw-ge. 🔩 😂 Get it? Ya get it??

scrooge

Ha-ha. Can we get this show on the road? 🚗

I learned a lot last night from Christmas Past, and I'm ready to learn more. 💡 📕

Send

ghost of christmas present

Pushy, pushy. But OK—that's what I'm here for anyway.

Tap on this.

scrooge

A robe?

ghost of christmas present

It's actually a kimono. 🙄 You need to get out more.

scrooge

✨ robe ✨

ghost of christmas present

Can you not? It's couture. Tap it!

Send

ghost of christmas present

✅ Ghost of Christmas Present and Scrooge have checked into a snowy street on Christmas Day.

ghost of christmas present

Check it out, Screw-ge! ❄️🎄🗑️🎋☃️🍎🍏🍒

scrooge

Wow. 🙄 Talk about #festive.

ghost of christmas present

Notice n-e-thang?

scrooge

Lots of people out and about buying things. 💳

ghost of christmas present

Yup! Prepping for Christmas dinner. 🍴👩‍👧

Send

scrooge

Everyone looks so . . . happy.

ghost of christmas present

Duh! Most people feel joy around Christmas.

scrooge

But they all look so, er, poor.

ghost of christmas present

They are. That's why they're all heading into bakeries.

Owners allow them to heat up their meals in their big ovens.

scrooge

Oh . . .

ghost of christmas present

Don't strain yourself thinking about it too hard.

I'm taking you somewhere else.

Send

ghost of christmas present

✓ Ghost of Christmas Present and Scrooge have checked into Bob Cratchit's 🏠.

scrooge

You brought me to Bob's?

ghost of christmas present

Check out this convo!

● ● ●

Chat transcript between Peter, Belinda, and Mrs. Cratchit
Peter: *It smells so good in the kitchen!* 👃🍗
Belinda: *Xmas rulez. We're gonna dine so fine.* 😀
Mrs. Cratchit: *Do you know when your father 🧔 and brother 👦 will be home from ⛪ ? They should be here soon. And where's your sister Martha?*

Send

• • •

mrs. cratchit

ETA?

martha

Be there any sec! 👣

mrs. cratchit

Yay! 💜 Why so late?

martha

Had a lot of work to finish up. NBD. Walking through the 🚪 in a few.

mrs. cratchit

Great. You can warm up by the 🔥 when you're here.

martha

I have a better idea! 💡

I'm gonna pretend I'm stuck at work and can't make it. 😉

mrs. cratchit

Martha!

Send

martha

It's just a little joke. 😉 Play along!

● ● ●

 Martha

The shop is crazy busy. 🌀 Not gonna make it 🏡 for Christmas. 🚫 🎅 😔 #IWontBeHomeForChristmas

👍 Mrs. Cratchit and 12 others like this.　　REPLY

Mrs. Cratchit: Boo! ☹️

Peter: We'll miss ya, sis.

👍 1 like

Belinda: #bummer

Bob Cratchit: WHAT, WHAT, WHAT! 😠

Martha: JK, Dad!! Gotcha. 😉 See you at home!

● ● ●

Bob cratchit

That was not a very nice trick our daughter just pulled. 😫 And I can't believe you played along! 😔

Send

Mrs. Cratchit

😂 I'm sorry. It was just too good to pass up!

Bob Cratchit

Lol. Anyway, I'm almost home. Tiny Tim 👲 is with me. Everyone else with you? Martha? 😉

Mrs. Cratchit

Yes, dear. How was Tim in church?

Bob Cratchit

A little like always.

Though he says the weirdest stuff sometimes. 😬 He said he hoped people saw his crutches today, so they'd be reminded that miracles can happen on Christmas. 🙏

Mrs. Cratchit

Oh, Tim. 😟

Bob Cratchit

It'll be fine. Let's get ready for the evening! 🎆

● ● ●

Send

Bob Cratchit

Sitting down to Christmas dinner 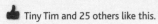 with my beautiful 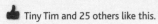!—feeling #blessed

👍 Tiny Tim and 25 others like this.   REPLY

Belinda: Xmas rulez!!

Peter: When can we open 🎁 🎁 🎁?

Mrs. Cratchit: 🍷

Tiny Tim: Gr8 pudding, Mom. 😃

Bob Cratchit: Merry Christmas to all! God bless us. 🤍

Tiny Tim: God bless us, every one!

👍 4 likes

Bob Cratchit

And cheers to Mr. Scrooge, who made this all possible!

 Be the first to like this.　　REPLY

Mrs. Cratchit: Scrooge! You know better than anyone else how awful that man is.
Bob Cratchit: It's Christmas, dear. Have a little cheer. 😉
Mrs. Cratchit: Oh, fine. To Scrooge's health, for your sake. And for the sake of Christmas. 🍷

👍 Bob, Tiny Tim, Peter, and Belinda like this.

scrooge

Will Tiny Tim live?! 😱

ghost of christmas present

Hate to break it to you, but— Ha! Get it? Break?

scrooge

 Send

ghost of christmas present

OK, OK, I know. #distasteful. He's not *totally* broken. 😃

But the future doesn't look so ☁ for him. 🔮 I see an empty stool in the corner with only one crutch propped up against it.

scrooge

No! 😔 You have to save him!

ghost of christmas present

I'm not Dr. Ghost of Christmas Present, ya know. 🏢 I can't save him.

Besides, why are you so upset? 🙁 You couldn't care less if these creatures—poor people 🦉—died. That's what you want, right? To put them in prisons and workhouses?

scrooge

😰😔

I thought I did, but now I feel 😷.

Send

ghost of christmas present

Buckle up, buddy. ✦ ✦ I've got one more place to show you. Tappity tap, tap, tap them.

✅ Ghost of Christmas Present and Scrooge have checked into Fred's .

ghost of christmas present

Remember how you treated your nephew?

scrooge

I'm afraid to. 😖

ghost of christmas present

Betcha thought that would his spirit.

scrooge

😞 I didn't mean for it to!

Send

ghost of christmas present

Calm down. 😌 You're not that important.

They'll prove it. Look 👀 and learn. 💡

● ● ●

fred

So excited for our party <u>tonight</u>! 🎉 🎈 🍸

fred's wife

me 2! 😘 do we have everything we need? drinks? 🍷

fred

✓

fred's wife

snax? 🍕

fred

✓

fred's wife

scrooge?

Send

Fred

🚫 Negative.

You should've heard Uncle Scrooge <u>today</u>! 😃 He said that Christmas was a humbug, LOL! And he believed it! 😂

Fred's wife

ugh. i can't even. he's tha worst. 😖

Fred

IDK. He's not so bad! Grumpy AF, yeah, but I ain't mad. 😎

Fred's wife

at least he's rich, amirite? 😍 💰 😍 💰

Fred

So? He might be rich, but it doesn't matter. 👎 He doesn't DO anything with it. Not for himself, and not for others. 😞 He's just wasting his life away.

Fred's wife

his loss! 💅

Send

Fred

It really is. Who suffers? He does! 😐 He doesn't like us, so he's not coming to our party. And he's going to miss out on a GREAT time! 🎁

Fred's wife

idk why we invite him every year. 👵 he always says no.

Fred

IDC. I'll keep trying anyway. He's not going to find 🔑 happiness in his gloomy office. ☁️ ☁️

Who knows—one year he might have a change of 🤍 and decide to come! Maybe he'll even give Bob Cratchit the day off and a raise. **$ $**

Fred's wife

lol. good 1! 😂

Fred

<u>Tonight</u> we cheers to Uncle Scrooge! 😏

Fred's wife

  to scrooge and his health! and a merry xmas!

Send

● ● ●

scrooge

Can we stay for the party? Please?! 🙏

Ghost of christmas present

Hello?? 👋 You know you can't interact with them.

Besides, I'm gettin' old. 👵

scrooge

Whaddya mean? 🙁 We just got started!

Ghost of christmas present

My time on 🌍 is running out. ⏳

I'm only . . . present (badumpsh) 😆 . . . until <u>midnight</u>.

scrooge

Oh. Is that when the last 👻 will visit me?

Ghost of christmas present

You got it. 👌

Send

ghost of christmas present

Before I leave, though, just remember if we've learned anything, it's that ignorance and greed are gonna bring you down. 💀

It's never too late to change, boo. 🐨

scrooge

TYVM for showing me everything <u>tonight</u>. It was eye-opening. 👀

ghost of christmas present

Aw, you ol' softie. 😊

GL2U, Screw-ge. 😉 TT4N!

● ● ●

 Scrooge

Can people change? Can you really teach an old dog new tricks? 🐵 🐶 I'm beginning to worry. —feeling stressed 😫

👍 Be the first to like this.   REPLY

Send

Chapter 4

Ghost of Christmas Yet to Come

ghost of christmas yet to come

scrooge

Hello? 🙁

ghost of christmas yet to come

scrooge

Are you the 👻 from the future?

ghost of christmas yet to come

scrooge

You must be. Past, present, and now you.

ghost of christmas yet to come

scrooge

This is starting to freak me out. 😣

But OK. Lead on, .

Send

ghost of christmas yet to come

scrooge

Seriously?! A skull?

ghost of christmas yet to come

✅ Ghost of Christmas Yet to Come and Scrooge have checked into a funeral parlor.

scrooge

A funeral? 😵 I'm not sure I'm ready for this. Who died?

ghost of christmas yet to come

Send

scrooge

You don't say much, do you?

ghost of christmas yet to come

scrooge

Oh, a guest list. Lemme see.

● ● ●

Send

💀 Ebenezer Scrooge—December 25 💀

Man Whom Scrooge Never Bothered to Speak To
> Comment: Does anyone know when he died? 💀

Woman Who Once Saw Him on the Street
> Comment: Last night—Xmas Eve 🎄

Lady Whom Scrooge Was Introduced to Three Times but Still Couldn't Remember
> Comment: How terrible! What did he . . . croak from? 🐸

Guy Who Doesn't Know How He Ended Up Here
> Comment: IDK, but I thought he'd never die! 😉

Man Who Has Only One Thing on His Mind
> Comment: What did he do with his 💰 💰 💰?

Woman Who Lived Around the Corner from Scrooge
> Comment: Not sure. 😕 Certainly didn't leave it to me!

● ● ●

Send

scrooge

Huh. IDGI. Are we at Jacob's funeral?

ghost of christmas yet to come

scrooge

Ya know, it'd be helpful if you actually said something once in a while.

ghost of christmas yet to come

scrooge

Fine.

✓ Scrooge and Ghost of Christmas Yet to Come have checked into a dirty, run-down shop in a bad part of town.

scrooge

Ew, this place is filthy.

Send

ghost of christmas yet to come

scrooge

Read this?

ghost of christmas yet to come

scrooge

Thanks. So helpful as always.

● ● ●

Transcript between Mrs. Dilber, Old Joe, Laundress, and Undertaker

Old Joe: Welcome, everyone. 👋

Mrs. Dilber: Let's get this started, shall we? I brought my goods. 📦 What about the rest of you?

Laundress: Got mine! 💼

Laundress: You sure it's OK to divvy up his things like this? 😯

Send

Mrs. Dilber: Completely. I used to scrub and clean his 🏠 all the time. I'm not even sure he knew that half this stuff existed. 😉 He won't miss any of it.

Laundress: True. He always took care of himself first. 😌

Mrs. Dilber: If he really wanted his belongings to go elsewhere after 💀, he would have been nicer to people, so someone could have taken care of him when he was 😷. Instead, he died alone.

Old Joe: And a dead man won't miss any of this.

Old Joe: I'll take the smallest 📦 first. Undertaker, whatcha got?

Undertaker: Err. ✏️ 📎 🔧

Old Joe: Okayyy. I'll pay 💰 for all of that. Next!

Laundress: 👕 👖 👚 👟 👢

Old Joe: Great. Here you are. 💰 💰 Next!

Mrs. Dilber: Open my 📦, Joe.

Old Joe: Let's see here. Wow! 😍

Old Joe: 👔

Old Joe: It's beautiful—looks never worn. 😨 How did you get this? It's very expensive.

Mrs. Dilber: I took it off of him, of course!

Old Joe: You took the 👔 off his back? Literally?

Send

Mrs. Dilber: Someone must have wanted him buried in it. 😂 What a waste! I replaced it with a different 👕. I took his curtains and bedsheets too. They're all yours.

Old Joe: 💰💰💰💰💰

scrooge

This is awful! 🙀 I've lived a life like that man. It could very well be me they're stealing from.

ghost of christmas yet to come

scrooge

Where to now? 👆

Send

Scrooge and Ghost of Christmas Yet to Come have
checked into a dark and dingy bedroom.

scrooge

Where are we?

ghost of christmas yet to come

scrooge

The bed? What's under the sheet?

ghost of christmas yet to come

scrooge

No. No, no, no, no, NO. I won't look!

Why isn't there anyone here grieving him?

Surely there has to be someone who misses him.
Show me someone who misses him!

Send

ghost of christmas yet to come

✅ Scrooge and Ghost of Christmas Yet to Come have checked into a lively 🏚️.

wife

Any news?? 📰 When will you be home?

Husband

Yes, but it's bad. 📥

wife

Let me guess. He didn't agree to extend our loan? 😖 I figured as much.

Husband

He's dead, 🏺. Heard it from his housekeeper firsthand.

wife

WTF?

Send

Husband

I thought he was just avoiding me, but it's true. He is 💀.

wife

But what about our debt?

Husband

I'm not completely sure, but . . . I don't think we have to worry about it anymore! 😀

wife

Really?! 😀 Finally! We can 😴 peacefully <u>tonight</u>. #MiraclesHappen

Husband

 Be home soon!

wife

😘😘

● ● ●

scrooge

Why would you show me people who are 😀😀 over this man's death??

Send

ghost of christmas yet to come

scrooge

Oh, no.

ghost of christmas yet to come

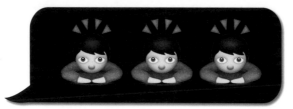

scrooge

OK, OK!

● ● ●

✓ Scrooge and Ghost of Christmas Yet to Come have checked into Bob Cratchit's 🏠.

scrooge

I don't think I like the reason you've brought me here.

Send

ghost of christmas yet to come

• • •

Group text: Peter, Belinda, Mrs. Cratchit, Bob Cratchit

peter

😭 It's not fair! When will you be home, Dad?

belinda

😭😭😭

peter

Why are you trying to one-up me? 😠

belinda

#Rude. I'm not. These tears are real. 💧💧

mrs. cratchit

Children, please. Now is not the time. 😔

bob cratchit

Your 👩 is right. We're in mourning. 😭

Send

Belinda

I'm sorry. I miss him, that's all. 😔

Peter

Me too. I miss .

Bob Cratchit

We all do. The funeral is set for <u>Sunday</u>.

Make sure you wear all black.

Mrs. Cratchit

I've been sewing 's all day. 😔

Bob Cratchit

I met Scrooge's nephew, Fred, <u>today</u>.

He had the nicest things to say and sends his thoughts and prayers to us.

Mrs. Cratchit

That was very nice of him, indeed. 😃

Send

Bob Cratchit

He gave me his card in case we ever need him.
I wouldn't be surprised if he helped Peter find a better job.

Peter

Really?! 😃 That would be amazing.

Mrs. Cratchit

Yes, it would! What a great man. 😍

Bob Cratchit

It's a ray of light in an otherwise bleak time.
We will never forget Tiny Tim.

Belinda

Never. #RestInPeaceTT

Mrs. Cratchit

😭

● ● ●

Ghost of Christmas Yet to Come

Send

scrooge

Our time is nearing the end, I know.

Tell me—I need to know whose funeral we attended. Please?

ghost of christmas yet to come

✅ Ghost of Christmas Yet to Come and Scrooge have checked into a cemetery.

ghost of christmas yet to come

scrooge

I'm afraid to 👀 whose name is on that headstone.

ghost of christmas yet to come

Send

scrooge

All right, sheesh! For someone so quiet, you sure are pushy.

ghost of christmas yet to come

scrooge

OMG

It was MY funeral??

This headstone has my name on it: EBENEZER SCROOGE.

ghost of christmas yet to come

scrooge

I've changed, though! I promise!

ghost of christmas yet to come

Send

scrooge

It's not too late, is it? Am I really ?

ghost of christmas yet to come

scrooge

I PROMISE to honor Christmas in my forever!

ghost of christmas yet to come

scrooge

Throughout the ENTIRE year.

I'll live in the past, present, and future. I won't forget everything I've learned from you three! 😓

ghost of christmas yet to come

Send

scrooge

Please make this headstone disappear.

I'll do anything. PLEASE!!!

Send

Chapter 5

Christmas Day

Scrooge

OMG. It's Christmas, and I'm still here!
 Pray for me that I make it through the whole day!—feeling relieved

👍 Be the first to like this.　　　REPLY

Scrooge: Hallelujah!
Scrooge: I'm so happy!!! 😀
Scrooge: So happy I'm crying!!!!! 😂
Scrooge: MERRY CHRISTMAS, EVERYONE!
MERRY CHRISTMAS! HAPPY NEW YEAR!
🎄🎁🎉🎈

● ● ●

scrooge

> Tell me, stranger—what day is it?!

555-1422

> New phone, who dis? ☹

scrooge

> A man living in the <u>past</u>, <u>present</u>, and <u>future</u>!

Send

555-1422

 Weirdo.

It's Christmas.

scrooge

Christmas! It's Christmas! MERRY CHRISTMAS!!!

● ● ●

scrooge

Good morning! ☀ Can you tell me if you've sold the large turkey that's been hanging in your window? 🦃

Grocer

The one that's as big as a small 👦?

scrooge

That's the one!

Grocer

Nope, still here. 🍴

Send

scrooge

Perfect! I'd like to buy it, please. 📟 I have the perfect 🏠 for it.

● ● ●

scrooge

Hello! 😃 I don't know if you remember me. This is Scrooge from Scrooge & Marley's. You contacted me the other day about donating 💵💵 to charity.

555-5586

yes, i remember. how r u?

scrooge

WONDERFUL! 🎉 AMAZING! ⭐ I hope you are too!

Did you collect a lot for the poor? 😊 What a wonderful thing you were doing. 😃

555-5586

r u SURE this is the same scrooge i spoke to? 🌀 😕 🌀

Send

scrooge

 my . It's me!

And I feel so awful for the way I treated you. 😔 I hope you'll still accept my donation for your charity. 💰💸💰💸

scrooge! 😍 it's too much. i don't know what to say! 🙈

scrooge

You don't need to say anything! 😌 Merry Christmas!!

● ● ●

✅ Scrooge has checked into Fred's .

scrooge

Fred! You 🏠? I'm right outside your 🚪!

fred

Uncle Scrooge? I can't believe you're here! 😯

Send

scrooge

I was wondering if your generous invitation to Christmas dinner with your 👨‍👩‍👧 was still open. I understand if you don't want me here, though. 😥

Fred

Of COURSE you're welcome! 😄 Merry Christmas, Uncle Scrooge! 😍

Send

Chapter 6

The Day After Christmas

✅ Scrooge has checked into Scrooge & Marley's.

scrooge

Do you know what time it is, Bob? 😠

bob cratchit

I'm so sorry, Mr. Scrooge! 😓 I know I'm running late!

scrooge

Twenty minutes late, to be specific. 🕐

bob cratchit

It won't happen again. 🙈

It's just because of yesterday's festivities. 🎉 🎁 🎅

scrooge

You're darn right it won't happen again. 😠 😤

bob cratchit

😔

scrooge

Because I'm giving you a raise!! 💰 ✅

Send

Bob Cratchit

Wh-what?

scrooge

Merry Christmas, Bob! You deserve this!

And I want to help your 👨‍👩‍👧 as much as I can too!

Bob Cratchit

You're really going to do that?

scrooge

I won't 😴 peacefully until we've found a cure 🏙️ for your precious Tiny Tim 🧒.

Bob Cratchit

Thank you, Mr. Scrooge! Thank you! Merry Christmas!

scrooge

Merry Christmas, Bob.

Merry Christmas to the whole 🌍!

Send

Scrooge

I've learned so much recently. 📚📝💡 About what it means to be rich 💰, but more important what it means to give. 💸💸💸 Most of all, though, I've learned how important friends and 👨‍👩‍👧 are, especially colleagues and nephews 👨 and children who still have so much life to experience 👶. Christmas is the most wonderful time of the year 🎄🎁🎅❄️💝 and its past, present, and future spirit 😌 should be recognized year-round. What a time to be alive!

👍 86 people have liked this.

REPLY

Send

Scrooge

I guess there's only one more thing to say—as someone 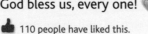 once wisely spoke:

God bless us, every one! 🤍

👍 110 people have liked this.   REPLY

Fred: We 🤍 you, Uncle Scrooge!

Bob Cratchit: You're the greatest 🎁 of all. 😀

Tiny Tim: Hey, cool! 😀

Ghost of Christmas Past: 🥒

Ghost of Christmas Present: That has nada to do w/xmas, GCP! ☹️

Ghost of Christmas Past: R U talking 2 urself? 😜

Ghost of Christmas Present: Goooood one. So clever. Better save 💾 that one for next year.

Ghost of Christmas Yet to Come: 👿

Ghost of Christmas Present: C'mon, GCYC! Lighten up already.

Ghost of Christmas Yet to Come: 💬

Ghost of Christmas Yet to Come: JK! MERRY CHRISTMAS, EVERYONE! 😉 🎉 🎄 🎁 🤍 🖤

Send

THe 411 for THose not in the know

411: Information

AF: As F*ck

BAE: Before Anyone Else (your babe)

FBF: Flashback Friday

FOMO: Fear Of Missing Out

GL2U: Good Luck To You

GR8: Great

IDC: I Don't Care

IDGI: I Don't Get It

IDK: I Don't Know

JK: Just Kidding

L8R: Later

NAGL: Not A Good Look

NBD: No Big Deal

NMF: Not My Fault

OMG: Oh My God

Send

OOTD: Outfit Of The Day

OTP: One True Pairing

RN: Right Now

TBH: To Be Honest

TBT: Throwback Thursday

TL;DR: Too Long; Didn't Read

TT4N: Ta Ta For Now

TTYN: Talk To You Never

TY: Thank You

TYVM: Thank You Very Much

WTF: What The F*ck

Y/Y: Yes/Yes

Send

Some emotions you might find in this book

Angry

Anguished

Annoyed

Anxious

Confused

Cool

Dead/Dying

Devilish

Devious

Disappointed

Embarrassed

Extremely amused (crying)

Extremely angry (fuming)

Extremely embarrassed

Extremely sad (crying)

Send

	Eyeroll
	Flirty
	Friendly (wink, wink)
	Goofy
	Happy
	Indifferent
	Love
	Panicked
	Sad
	Shocked
	Shocked and screaming
	Sick
	Silly
	Sleepy
	Speechless
	Tearing up
	Teasing
	Unamused
	Worried

Send

BRETT WRIGHT has a BFA in creative writing and works full-time as a children's book editor in New York City. In college, he studied Shakespearean tragedy, which was sadly lacking in emoticons. He loves receiving 📚 during the holidays. 😉 @brettwright

CHARLES DICKENS was an English writer born in 1812. His best-known works are *Oliver Twist, Great Expectations, A Tale of Two Cities,* and, of course, *A Christmas Carol.* He was a popular writer during his lifetime, producing fifteen novels, five novellas, and hundreds of short stories and articles. He is still recognized today as a literary genius. 📚

Send

FOMO?

Read on for a peek at

Mrs. Bennet

 **Top 5 Things Rich Men Want**
[TeaFeed article]
1. A Wife

Click to read!

 REPLY

Lady Lucas: Duh, everyone knows that!

 ✓ Mr. Bingley has checked into Netherfield Park.

 Mrs. Bennet, Lady Lucas, and 20 others like this.

Mrs. Bennet

OMG, babe, guess who just bought Netherfield Park!

Charles Bingley

Send

Mr. Bennet

Single or married?

Mrs. Bennet

SINGLE!! 😀 Will you go see him? 🦌

Mr. Bennet

👎

Mrs. Bennet

What?! Why not?!?! 😖

Mr. Bennet

Go without me. My fingers are crossed for Lizzy! 💍

Mrs. Bennet

Lizzy?! 😯 But Jane's the prettiest! 👰 And Lydia's the most fun! 😜 I don't know why you 🤍 Lizzy the most....

Send

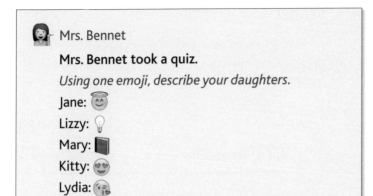

Mrs. Bennet

Mrs. Bennet took a quiz.
Using one emoji, describe your daughters.
Jane: 😇
Lizzy: 💡
Mary: 📓
Kitty: 😍
Lydia: 😘

👍 Kitty likes this.

REPLY

Mrs. Bennet

I'm so over Bingley!! He just moved in 🏠 & it's all anyone talks about anymore!! 😴

Mr. Bennet

If I knew you were 😷 of him, I wouldn't have gone over there this morning. 😉

Mrs. Bennet

WHAT?! OMG! Best husband everrr!!! 🤍

Send

Mrs. Bennet

Lady Lucas, what did your husband say about Mr. Bingley?!?! I need details!!

Lady Lucas

Young! Handsome! Charming! #AllTheThings

And that he'll be GOING TO OUR BALL.

Mrs. Bennet

OMG!!! We'll be there!

🎉 Dancer 🎉

 Charles Bingley asks Charlotte Lucas to dance.

 Charlotte Lucas accepts. #SwipesRight ⊗ ♥

 Charles Bingley asks Jane Bennet to dance.

 Jane Bennet accepts. #SwipesRight ⊗ ♥

Send

Charles Bingley asks
Jane Bennet to dance again.

 Jane Bennet accepts.
#SwipesRight ⓧ 🤍

 Charles Bingley suggests
Fitzwilliam Darcy ask
Elizabeth Bennet to dance.

 Fitzwilliam Darcy declines.
#SwipesLeft Ⓧ 🤍

↪ Bingley: Darcy, c'mon! Ur
really not going to dance with
anyone?

Darcy: Your sisters are all taken.
None of these other girls are
good enough 4 me. 👎
You got the prettiest 1. 😇

Bingley: I know, right?
#SorryNotSorry

Bingley: But her sister Lizzy
seems cool.

Darcy: Meh. Not hot. Besides, if
no1 else wants her, why should I?

Bingley: You are the WORST
wingman. 😔

Send

Jane

Lizzy, dance w/ that hot guy Darcy!

Lizzy

Look at your Dancer feed. He's a jerk.

Jane

Maybe it was an accidental swipe left?! 😕

Lizzy

Whatevs. I won't let a guy like that ruin my night.

 Mrs. Bennet

OMG such a fun night! Bingley and Jane danced twice! Not the first dance (damn you, Charlotte Lucas! Lol jk jk). But still, TWICE! 😍 OH!!! And this other guy, Darcy, was a complete 🐷 to everyone all night long. He didn't even dance with Lizzy!!! Lame!

👍   REPLY

Mr. Bennet: Everyone please disregard the above. There's nothing to here. . . .

Send

jane

Lizzy, I think I'm in love <3 <3 <3

I can't believe Bingley asked me to dance—twice!  😊 😊 😊

Lizzy

I can. 😃 Do you have any idea how pretty you are? Hint: ✅ 😉

Bingley's sisters, though . . . 😬

jane

Mrs. Hurst & Miss Bingley?

Lizzy

Yeah . . . #Yikes 🙈 They think they're hot sh*t, huh? 😏

jane

Maybe they're not so bad once you get 2 know them.

Lizzy

😂 😂 😂 Hopefully I'll never have to!

Send

Jane

> Charlotte, Mr. Bingley danced with you first!

charlotte

> But he danced with you twice! 🍀

> Darcy really should have danced with Lizzy.

Lizzy

> He had me on his Not Hot list, that's for sure.
> I needed an extra shawl for all that #Shade.

charlotte

> SMH. Ya, he's stuck up. But let's be real . . . he has reason
> 2 b, with his 💰 and everything else going for him.

Lizzy

> I'd be cool with his pride if he didn't trample
> on mine. #HatersGonnaHate

Send